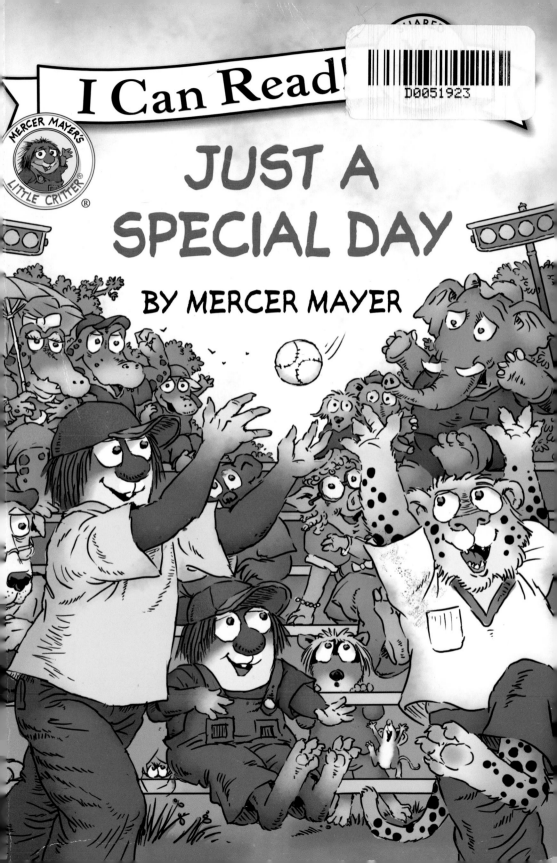

HOORAY!

_____

can read this book!

www.harpercollinschildrens.com
BOOK NEWS, GAMES, CONTESTS, AND MORE

US $3.99 / $4.99 CAN
ISBN 978-0-06-147817-8

Dear Parent:
Your child's love of reading starts here!

Every child learns to read in a different way and at his or her own speed. Some go back and forth between reading levels and read favorite books again and again. Others read through each level in order. You can help your young reader improve and become more confident by encouraging his or her own interests and abilities. From books your child reads with you to the first books he or she reads alone, there are I Can Read Books for every stage of reading:

SHARED READING
Basic language, word repetition, and whimsical illustrations, ideal for sharing with your emergent reader

BEGINNING READING
Short sentences, familiar words, and simple concepts for children eager to read on their own

READING WITH HELP
Engaging stories, longer sentences, and language play for developing readers

READING ALONE
Complex plots, challenging vocabulary, and high-interest topics for the independent reader

ADVANCED READING
Short paragraphs, chapters, and exciting themes for the perfect bridge to chapter books

I Can Read Books have introduced children to the joy of reading since 1957. Featuring award-winning authors and illustrators and a fabulous cast of beloved characters, I Can Read Books set the standard for beginning readers.

A lifetime of discovery begins with the magical words "I Can Read!"

Visit www.icanread.com for information
on enriching your child's reading experience.

JUST A SPECIAL DAY

BY MERCER MAYER

HARPER

An Imprint of HarperCollinsPublishers

To Harlan Christenson.
Welcome to the world!

I Can Read Book® is a trademark of HarperCollins Publishers.

ISBN 978-0-06-207198-9 (trade bdg.) — ISBN 978-0-06-147817-8 (pbk.)

15 16 17 18 PC/WOR 10 9 8 7 6 5 ❖ First Edition

A Big Tuna Trading Company, LLC/J. R. Sansevere Book
www.littlecritter.com

Mom and Little Sister
have to go to town.
Dad and I stay home.

We will have a special day
just Dad and me.
Mom gives us a list of chores.

We will clean the kitchen
just for Mom.
But that isn't much fun.

We ride bicycles to the
park instead.

Dad throws the football.
I run to catch it.

I say, "I'm sorry."

"I'm hungry," I say.

We get hot dogs.

Mine has too much mustard.

My clothes are messy.

Dad takes me to the water
fountain to clean me up.

13

I have a leftover hot dog bun.

I will feed the fish.

I throw it in the pond.

Oops. Now all the fish are
coming to me.
The fishermen are not happy.

Dad says, "I have an idea.
Let's go to the ballpark
and watch a game."

The batter hit a foul ball.
Up and up it went. Then down
and down it came.

"I will catch it for you,"
Dad says.

Dad misses the catch and now
he needs a doctor. Poor Dad!

The doctor takes a look at Dad.

He fixes Dad up.

We leave.

We go home.

I think Dad got too excited.

"Dad," I say, "today was fun.
You just rest and I will finish
our chores for Mom."

Dad falls asleep.

I fill the dishwasher.

I fill the washing machine.

It needs lots of soap.

I fold the laundry.

"Dad, wake up and see
what I did to help," I say.

I ask, "Are you happy
that I helped, Dad?"

Dad gives me a hug.

I give my dad a hug.

"Hooray," I say.

"Mom and Little Sister are home."

Mom asks, "What kind of day did you boys have?"

I say, "It was just a special day.
Right, Dad?"